Felix and His Flying Machine

Lee Aucoin, *Creative Director*
Jamey Acosta, *Senior Editor*
Heidi Fiedler, *Editor*
Produced and designed by
Denise Ryan & Associates
Illustration © Clare Elsom
Rachelle Cracchiolo, *Publisher*

Teacher Created Materials
5301 Oceanus Drive
Huntington Beach, CA 92649-1030
http://www.tcmpub.com
Paperback: ISBN: 978-1-4333-5604-9
Library Binding: ISBN: 978-1-4807-1726-8
© 2014 Teacher Created Materials

Written by
Sally Odgers

D1509570

by
n

Contents

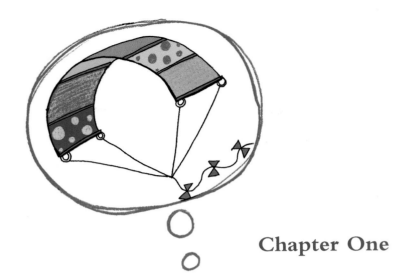

Chapter One

Felix O' Finnegan and the Start of Things

Felix O'Finnegan was born with big ideas. When he was a baby, he found a skateboard under the stairs. He rode it out the front door and down to the river. His mother caught him just in time.

"Felix O'Finnegan! What are you doing?" cried Mrs. O'Finnegan. She carried him into the house and found his building blocks. "Play with these instead," she said.

Felix built a tower taller than he was. But then his father came home.

"Hello, Felix!" said Mr. O'Finnegan as he banged the door behind him. The tower teetered. It tottered. And finally, it toppled. Felix stuck out his bottom lip and yelled. Then, he built the tower again, only better.

Felix grew, and so did his big ideas. He climbed the highest tree in the park, trying to reach the clouds. His mother caught him just in time.

"Felix O'Finnegan! Come down from there right now!" cried Mrs. O'Finnegan. She led him into the house and gave him paper and pencils. "Play with these instead."

Felix unraveled his sweater and used the yarn and his pencils to build a kite. He sent it soaring up into the clouds. But then his father came home.

"Hello, Felix!" said Mr. O'Finnegan. He pulled the window shut. The kite flipped and flopped. Then, it flapped and fell. Felix frowned. Then, he built another kite, only better.

Chapter Two

Felix Finds His Feet

When he was five, it was time for Felix to go to school. Felix was excited. He knew it would be an adventure.

"I hope Felix fits in at school," said his father.

"I hope school fits in with Felix," said his mother.

Felix filled his bag with useful things and studied hard. He worked with numbers and wrote down new ideas.

Mr. Armitage was pleased with Felix. He gave him a smiley sticker. Felix finished his work, lickety split. And he asked the teacher a lot of questions. "What did dinosaurs eat for breakfast? How do helicopters fly? What happens if you freeze a lemon for fifty years?"

"Felix O'Finnegan, I don't know!" Mr. Armitage sighed. "Play with these instead." He sent Felix to The Busy Box.

The Busy Box was filled with wheels and gears, plastic nuts and bolts. Felix built a pair of enormous roller skates that could hold six kids. They zipped and zagged wildly around the playground.

Mr. Armitage found them heading for the gate. "Feeee-lix!" yelled Mr. Armitage.

The children stopped short and toppled down like dominoes. Mr. Armitage caught them just in time.

Felix sighed. Mr. Armitage sighed. The other children sighed, too.

"Felix, why did you do that?" asked Mr. Armitage as he pulled the wheels off the enormous skates.

Felix shrugged. "I had a big idea. I wanted to see if it would work."

"Big ideas are good," said Mr. Armitage. "But ask a grown-up *before* you try them out."

"Okay," said Felix.

Mr. Armitage smiled.

Chapter Three

Felix and His Flying Machine

After that, Felix asked grown-ups about his big ideas. There was only one problem. Grown-ups often said no.

"*No*, Felix," said his mother when he wanted to turn her mixer into a helicopter.

"*No*, Felix," said his father when he wanted to attach a propeller to the car.

"*No*, Felix," said Mr. Armitage when he wrote about a fabulous flying machine.

"I didn't ask to make it. I only wrote about it on the computer," said Felix.

"I know," said Mr. Armitage, "but you wrote about how to make it, and that makes me nervous."

"Don't you think it would work?" asked Felix.

"I *hope* it won't work," said Mr. Armitage. "Felix O'Finnegan, you are *not* to make a flying machine at school."

Chapter Four

Felix Flies

"Okay, I won't make a flying machine at school," said Felix. And he didn't—he made it at home.

Felix built his flying machine in the attic. He had already asked a grown-up. So he didn't bother to ask his mom and dad.

"Where is Felix?" asked Mr. O'Finnegan one rainy Saturday night.

"He went upstairs," said Mrs. O'Finnegan. "I hope it's sunny tomorrow."

"The weather report said it will rain all week," said Mr. O'Finnegan.

"Oh, bother," said Mrs. O'Finnegan. "I wanted to work in the garden."

Up in the attic, Felix fastened the final knot. He tested the fins and flipped the propeller. The engine hummed gently. Felix smiled, switched it off, and hurried down to supper.

The rain poured all night. It poured all week. The river rose higher and higher.

Mr. O'Finnegan worried when the water crept into the kitchen. "We'll have to go somewhere safe," he said.

"It's too late," said Mrs. O'Finnegan. "The car is underwater and we don't have a boat."

"We'll call for help," said Mr. O'Finnegan. "I'll make some sandwiches."

Felix grinned. "I've got an idea! Come on. It's time to rescue ourselves." His mom and dad followed him up the stairs.

In the attic, Felix opened the window. He packed up his parents and flipped on the propeller. The flying machine chugged to life. With a jolt, it lifted off. And they soared out of the attic. Over the water they flew, off to higher ground.

The next day, the flying machine was on the news, but Felix didn't notice. He had an idea for a time machine. He wanted to learn what dinosaurs ate for breakfast.

Sally Odgers is an award-winning author who lives in Tasmania, Australia. She lives in a house full of books, music, and Jack Russell terriers. Sally wrote *Journey to the Center of the Earth, Where Did the Dinosaurs Go?* and *The Untold Story of Ms. Mirabella* for Read! Explore! Imagine! Fiction Readers.

Clare Elsom loves drawing mischievous characters just like Felix! She also illustrated *Soo Yun's Book* for Read! Explore! Imagine! Fiction Readers.